Tom T's
Hat
Rack

Tom T's Hat Rack

A Story About Paying it Forward

WRITTEN BY
Michele Spry

ILLUSTRATED BY PEGGY A. GUEST

Proceeds from this book will be donated to
the American Cancer Society

DEDICATED TO TOM TRABUE.

CHAPTER ONE

Shelby Summers attended Eagle Ridge Elementary School as a 4th (almost 5th!) grader. Shelby's mom, Karen, was a nurse at Sunnyvale Children's Hospital, and Shelby's dad, John, was a doctor at Clarkson's Cancer Hospital.

Shelby didn't have any brothers or sisters to play with, so she spent her days after school and all summer with Tom and Kim Tucker, a retired couple that lived only four houses away.

Mr. and Mrs. T, as Shelby always thought of them, were as close as grandparents to Shelby, and she and her parents spent lots of time at their house. Everyone became such good friends that they thought of each other like family. It became a tradition to have dinners together three nights a week, and Mr. and Mrs. T took care of Shelby while her parents were at work.

Mr. T was an average sized man with a full head of silver hair and always wore a hat when he worked outside in the garden.

Mrs. T had gray curls that bounced when she laughed, and big blue eyes that seemed to smile all on their own.

The last day of school for the year had almost arrived, and Shelby couldn't wait to start her summer break. Lots of her friends would be going on family summer vacations, but not Shelby - she was looking forward to spending the summer with Mr. and Mrs. T. Other than her parents, they were the next best thing for Shelby to spend time with as they were the only family Shelby had around here. The rest of Shelby's family, her aunt, uncles, and cousins, lived way out on the other side of the country, and the Summers family didn't see them as often as they'd like. But Shelby didn't mind - Mr. and Mrs. T were her world, and she liked it that way!

Shelby had made a deal with her mom and dad that if she stayed home during the summer they would all take a family trip for Christmas break to her cousins in Arizona. Her parents had promised they could go somewhere warm while it was cold and snowy which sounded awesome! Besides, Shelby loved the summer, swimming with her friends, playing baseball, riding bikes, and fishing at the creek.

CHAPTER TWO

The last week of school before summer started, Shelby spent lots of time with her friends and favorite teachers. She made sure she talked to each of her past teachers, telling them how much fun 4th grade was but that she really missed their classrooms too.

First, Shelby went to Mrs. Robbins, her kindergarten teacher. Just as soon as she stepped through the door, Mrs. Robbins said, "Well, here comes the most adorable, curly headed, green eyed girl that I've ever I had in my classroom."

Shelby smiled from ear to ear. She loved talking to her teachers, and they always had something nice to say.

"Shelby, you can stop by my 2nd grade classroom anytime you like," said Mrs. Carter, *another* one of Shelby's favorite teachers. When she'd finished saying hello to every single one of them, she skipped out to the playground to join her class.

Outside stood Mrs. Gentry, the school principal with the funniest, sweetest smile of them all. "Hi Mrs. G!" Shelby said, and gave a big wave.

"Did you have a good school year, Shelby?" asked Mrs. Gentry.

"I sure did! And now, I'm looking forward to…" Just before she could finish the school bell went Riiiiiing. "Wow! I've got to go back to class Mrs. G… Bye!" and she skipped back inside.

Mrs. Gentry smiled to herself, and softly said, "Bye, Shelby!" as she walked to her office.

As Shelby and her friends rode the bus home that day they talked and giggled. "One more day of school!" the girls all said. They hooked their index fingers together and raised them in the air. "Friends forever!" they cried just as the bus got to Shelby's stop.

"Bye, I'll see you tomorrow," said Shelby, and she jumped off the bus and headed over to Mr. and Mrs. T's house.

"Well, hello Shelby. How was school today?" Mrs. T asked with a twinkle in her eyes as Shelby sat up on a stool at the bar in the kitchen. Mrs. T pulled a fresh tray of hot peanut butter cookies out of the oven.

"How did you know peanut butter cookies are my favorite?" Shelby asked, her eyes round and sparkling. She couldn't wait to eat one with a big glass of milk.

"You've been coming to our house almost every day for the last ten years and let's just say I've taken notes, Shelby." Mrs. T winked at her.

Mr. T stepped into the kitchen. "I smell cookies and hear talking so I thought I would see who stopped by."

Shelby hopped off her stool and gave him a big hug. She and Mr. T were nearly inseparable, and they'd seen each other almost every single day for the last ten years.

"Shelby was just getting ready to tell me about her day," said Mrs. T. She stacked cookies on a plate and poured each of them a big glass of milk, then they all went into the dining room and sat down at the big table.

"School was so much fun today because I went to see Mrs. Carter and Mrs. Robbins," said Shelby, in between bites

of delicious hot cookie. "I'll see Miss Westbrook and Mrs. Peterson tomorrow to say goodbye and tell them that I'll see them next year. I am a little sad that school will be over, but only a little bit! I'm more excited about spending time with you and Mr. T while mom and dad are at work."

Shelby could tell that Mr. T liked the peanut butter cookies just as much as she did. He was on his second one already!

A familiar "hoooonk" came from outside, as Shelby's mom waited in the car for her out in the street. "Oh! I've gotta go but I'll see you guys tomorrow after school!" Shelby took a last sip of milk, wiped her mouth on her napkin, and skipped out to get in the car with her mother.

Chapter Three

"Shelby, it's time to get up and get ready for your last day of 4th grade," said her dad in a sing-song, gentle voice. He poked his head into her room. "Your mom has your breakfast ready downstairs."

"Okay, dad. I'll be right there." She sprung out of bed, put on her favorite dress, which she'd laid out specially the night before, brushed her hair and teeth, and headed downstairs. Today was her last day as a 4th grader and she was excited to see her friends and teachers.

"Thanks, mom," she said after she finished her cereal. "I'll see you this afternoon at Mr. and Mrs. T's house for dinner… Love you!" She grabbed her backpack and left the house. The screen door banged behind her as she skipped out to the bus stop.

At the beginning of class that day, Mrs. Sappington, Shelby's teacher, told the students how proud of them she was. "You're becoming such wonderful young men and women," she said. "Your manners have improved so much, and you've really worked together as a team to get projects done throughout the year." Shelby felt so grown-up and proud, and everyone in the class was focused on what their teacher was saying.

Mrs. Sappington asked if anyone had anything they would like to share about what they were doing for summer break.

Mikel raised his hand first. "I'm going to Texas to see my Aunt Cheryl and Uncle Greg for the summer."

"I'm going with my family to Boston," said Jaxon who sat two seats away from Shelby. "We're going to visit the museums, walk the Freedom Trail and take in a baseball game at Fenway Park."

"My family and I will be traveling to India for three weeks to see my grandparents," said Amita.

"Those are great plans, everyone," Mrs. Sappington said. "Shelby, what are you going to do this summer?"

"We're going to Arizona at Christmas, and I am going to

spend the summer with Mr. and Mrs. T." said Shelby. She didn't mind at all that she wasn't traveling anywhere over the summer since she knew her mom and dad both had patients that needed them and she was in good hands with Mr. and Mrs. T.

"You know there is nothing wrong staying close to home for summer break," said Mrs. Sappington.

Riiiiiing went the recess bell. "I'll see you guys and gals in twenty minutes," said Mrs. Sappington as they all got up to play.

As Shelby walked out the classroom door, she heard the sweetest voice. "Well good morning, Shelby. You look very pretty today." It was Miss Westbrook, Shelby's first grade teacher.

"Miss Westbrook," said Shelby, "you are the sweetest teacher and I wanted to come give you a hug and say goodbye for the school year. I really miss being in your classroom, but I am glad you are just down the hall so I can come say hello."

"Shelby, you can come visit me whenever you want. Don't forget, Bugsy the bunny loves to see you too." Miss Westbrook gave Shelby a big smile as Shelby went to go play tag with her friends.

Later, just as Shelby's 4th grade class was about to come to an end and the summer break begin, Mrs. Sappington let them know she was going to be teaching their 5th grade class next year. Everyone clapped and cheered. It wasn't just Shelby who enjoyed her class, everyone did!

Mrs. Sappington quickly got everyone to quiet down and then gave them a little homework to do over the summer. Shelby heard some of the students say things like "Oh man, I don't want to do homework over the summer." "Do we have to?" or "Do we get extra credit?"

Mrs. Sappington let everyone know it would be an easy project and she would feature the best one on the bulletin board for one month at the start of the new school year. Shelby couldn't wait to hear what the homework was! She enjoyed a challenge and loved her school work.

"The project," said Mrs. Sappington, "is for each student to write a story about something you did over the summer that forever changed your life for the better. Something you did that you won't ever forget." Shelby could hear whispers throughout the classroom as some of the students thought ahead about the things they would write before they even experienced it.

Shelby loved writing and couldn't wait for this challenge. She wasn't sure what the summer would bring, but she was ready to enjoy it with some of her most favorite people!

Riiiiiing went the school bell for the last time that school year!

"Have a great summer everyone and don't forget your homework!" said Mrs. Sappington. Shelby ran up and gave her a big hug. Then she quickly ran to catch up with her friends and head for the bus. Summer break had just begun!

CHAPTER FOUR

The bus pulled up to Shelby's stop and Mr. and Mrs. T were outside waiting for her. "There's our girl," said Mrs. T as Shelby leapt down the steps and gave her a hug. "Are you ready to start your summer vacation?"

"You bet I am," said Shelby. "But first can we have our after school snack together?" This was a tradition they had since Shelby started school. Mr. and Mrs. T were always so eager to hear about Shelby's friends, her school work, and whatever else was going on at school as a way to remain active in Shelby's life. And she loved telling them everything she could think of, all while enjoying wonderful baked cookies.

"I love coming to your house every day," said Shelby. "I just couldn't imagine life without you living just down the street. I love you guys," Shelby said with a shy smile.

" We love you, too," Mrs. T said with the warmest smile you've ever seen. Mr. T nodded and cleared his throat. He was manly, but Shelby meant the world to him, and she knew it.

Shelby hugged them both. She was ready to start telling Mr. and Mrs. T every single detail about her last day of school; she was so excited to tell them Mrs. Sappington would be her 5th grade teacher next year, too. But just as she was about to speak, Shelby's mom and dad drove up into Mr. and Mrs. T's driveway.

"Well, good afternoon!" said Shelby's dad. He lifted some grocery bags out of the car.

Her mom called, "We brought a few groceries to help make dinner tonight."

Mrs. T said, "Shelby, why don't you tell us about your last day of school while we get dinner going?"

No one else could get a word in while Shelby told them all about her day. It was as if she couldn't get the words out fast enough. Within ten minutes, they all knew how Shelby felt about everything: she was so excited for summer to start- she was a little sad that she wouldn't see most of her friends for three whole months- there was a writing assignment for the summer... Whew!

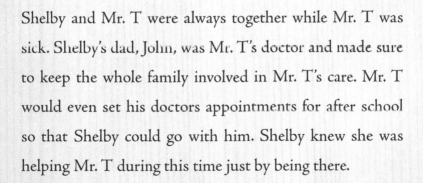

Mostly, this summer was going to be special for Shelby for the best reason - she would get to spend lots of time with Mr. T. Last September, Mr. T had been diagnosed with cancer. For six months he had gone through chemotherapy every other week, and for one month he went for radiation every single day. Sometimes he felt really sick and Shelby had stuck by his side to make sure he ate good meals and took his medicine on time. She would color in coloring books by his bedside when he didn't feel the best and take a walk with him when he felt better.

Shelby and Mr. T were always together while Mr. T was sick. Shelby's dad, John, was Mr. T's doctor and made sure to keep the whole family involved in Mr. T's care. Mr. T would even set his doctors appointments for after school so that Shelby could go with him. Shelby knew she was helping Mr. T during this time just by being there.

Everyone agreed to allow Shelby to be involved in Mr. T's care. She was old enough to understand this was happening to someone very close to her and wanted to be as much

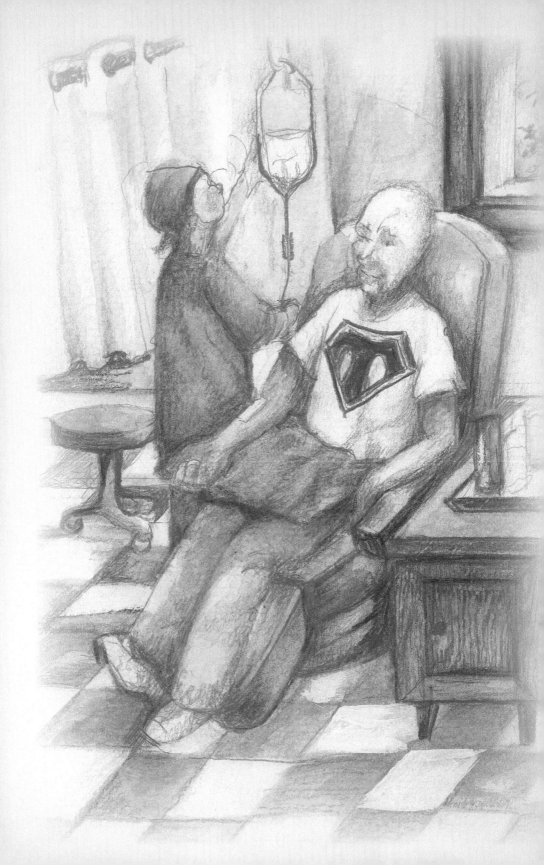

help as she could. The patients and staff around Clarkson's Cancer Center got to know Shelby and loved the positive outlook she brought to everybody she met while keeping Mr. and Mrs. T company during Mr. T's treatments.

Shelby often colored pages or made little crafts for other patients because she knew it helped to take their minds off their treatments. It was something she enjoyed and she loved the way it made people smile.

Because of all this, Shelby knew that her time with Mr. T was very precious. She knew this summer would be something special, and even magical, and she couldn't wait.

CHAPTER FIVE

Mr. and Mrs. T would often talk about Shelby after she had gone home. They loved her caring spirit and that she always enjoyed doing things for others and never thinking about herself. They were so proud of the young lady she had become and were so happy to have her as a part of their lives. Many times they would walk over to John and Karen's house after Shelby went to bed so they could talk about life, health, and of course, Shelby.

Tonight, Mr. T talked about how wanted to have Shelby help him with a little project. After going through these tough health issues with his cancer, he decided to do something positive to benefit others. He knew with Shelby's caring heart, and vision to help people, he and Shelby would be able to accomplish this idea over summer break. He told her parents all about it, and they were so excited about it they readily agreed not to say anything to Shelby. They would let it be a surprise from Mr. T.

Next day, the first morning of summer break, Shelby burst into Mr. and Mrs. T's kitchen. "Good morning, Mrs. T!" she chirped. "Today is the first day of my summer vacation and we have the whole day together. What would you like to do?"

Just then, Mr. T entered the kitchen. "Well, Shelby, I'm glad you asked." He winked at Mrs. T. "I have a little project I would like you to help me with."

Mr. and Mrs. T sat down at the table with Shelby as she ate her cinnamon toast. "I have an idea," explained Mr. T. "I need *your* help to make it possible. I can't tell you what it is exactly, because it's a surprise. But as we go through each part of the project, I'll explain what we are doing. One thing I can tell you - it's going to be something we can take pride in that will make others happy."

Shelby swallowed the last bite of her toast and said, "Of course I'll help, but I have two questions. Question number one: When do we start? Question number two: Is Mrs. T' going to help us?" Mr. T looked at Mrs. T and smiled. Shelby never failed to amaze him, always thinking about everyone else.

"We can start today if you like Shelby, and Mrs. T will make sure to keep our bellies full with great lunches and afternoon snacks. But this will be our project. Just you and me."

He waited for Shelby to finish her milk, then they went into the garage to see what he would need to buy when they went to town. "Shelby, would you grab a notebook and pencil please, so we can make our list?" asked Mr. T.

Shelby grabbed a notebook and wrote down every single item that Mr. T rattled off, as fast as she could.

"Twelve 4-by-4 inch oak posts that are 6 foot long, ten 2-by-4 inch oak boards that are 8 foot long, 48 decorative hooks, wood glue, 5 pounds of 2 1/2-inch wood screws, wood putty, wood stain (medium oak), #150 grit sand paper, 1 gallon of polyurethane, and red rope lickorish."

Mr. T loved red rope licorice and he knew Shelby did, too.

Mr. T wanted to teach Shelby how to write it properly, like an engineer, for Mr. Baxter at the hardware store. "Write it in a list, now, like this:

1. (12) 4 x 4 oak posts, 6' long

2. (10) 2 x 4 oak boards, 8' long

3. (48) decorative hooks

4. wood glue

5. 5 lbs of 2 1/2" wood screws

6. wood putty

7. wood stain (medium oak)

8. #150 grit sand paper

9. 1 gallon polyurethane

10. and red rope licorice. That's l-i-c-o-r-i-c-e."

Mr. T cleared his throat. "Good! I have a skill saw, tape measure, square, contractor's pencils, and saw horses. Ok, Shelby, now that we have our list, let's go to town after lunch and get our supplies."

CHAPTER SIX

With their list in hand Mr. T and Shelby climbed in the truck and headed to Baxter's Hardware Store.

"Well hello Mr. Baxter. How's business going today?" asked Mr. T.

"Business is good when I have great people like you that support my store," said Mr. Baxter. He was an older gentleman with thick gray hair, and Shelby knew he took pride in making his customers happy. The sign above the store said Mr. Baxter's father had started this hardware store in 1928, and that it had unique items you can't find anywhere else.

"Shelby and I are working on a little project and need to get a few items," said Mr. T. "Shelby, lets grab a cart and see what we can find."

Shelby and Mr. T laughed and told jokes and were so happy together they were like two peas in a pod. As they wandered through the hardware store aisles, they heard Mr. Baxter helping other customers who had walked in.

"He's such a wonderful person in our community and loves working in his hardware store," Mr. T told Shelby as she pushed the cart past the biggest pile of nails she'd ever seen. "He had some health problems over the years, but all the time he's worked here I bet he hasn't missed a total of twenty days. That is dedication and commitment, two great qualities you have, Shelby."

Shelby swelled up with pride and had a huge smile on her face as they headed up to the checkout counter to pay for their materials. "Did you all find everything you needed?" said Mr. Baxter.

"We (pant) sure (pant) did," said Shelby as she sloooowly pushed the heavy cart to the counter. It was a bear to push with all the things Mr. T had piled inside, but Shelby insisted. "Mr. T and I are working on a surprise project for the summer."

"Well, it looks like it will take a little while to finish your project with all this stuff." Mr. Baxter smiled at her. "But when you are done, please come back to the store and tell me what you made. Okay, Shelby?"

"Of course we'll come back and tell you all about it," Shelby said as they walked out the door. "See you later Mr. Baxter." She gave him a big wave.

Mrs. T stood in the sun watering the flowers in her yard when Mr. T and Shelby pulled back in the driveway. "It looks like you two bought out Mr. Baxter's whole hardware store with all of that stuff in the bed of the truck," she chuckled.

"We got everything on our list, and even some licorice," said Shelby.

"Shelby," said Mr. T, "tomorrow we will unload all of our supplies, but it's almost time for dinner! Let's go wash our hands and wait for your mom and dad to get here." He headed inside.

Chapter Seven

The next morning Shelby was up bright and early ready to work on the project. She gave her mom and dad a quick kiss and a hug before she headed out the door to Mrs. and Mrs. T's house. As she ran out the house, excited to get started on their project, she nearly tripped and realized she'd forgotten to tie her tennis shoes. She kneeled down on the front porch, quickly tied her shoes, and ran to Mrs. and Mr. T's house as fast as she could.

"Good morning!" Shelby said in their doorway as she tried to catch her breath.

"Shelby," said Mrs. T, "You must be excited to start that project. You're never here until 7:30 and today you're twenty minutes early - but you know you are always welcome any time of day." Mrs. T started making her some breakfast. "Mr. T will be right back. He had to run up to the grocery store to get a few things for dinner tonight."

Shelby made herself comfortable at the table, and Mrs. T placed a plate of delicious cinnamon toast in front of her. Just then Mr. T pulled into the driveway. Shelby snatched up a piece of toast and said, "Thank you for breakfast, Mrs. T. I've got to go help Mr. T." She hurried and ate the last bite of her cinnamon toast, then she ran into the garage to meet him.

"Good morning Mr. T," she said as he got out of the car. "I've eaten breakfast and am all ready to get started on our project!"

"Whoa, there! That's great, Shelby," he said grinning at her. "I just need to take the groceries inside first." When he came back out, they unloaded all the materials they had bought yesterday. Shelby couldn't believe how much they had. Wood and nails and all kinds of fun things.

They placed everything in neat, separate piles in the garage, because this would become their workshop for the next several weeks. Because Mr. T had worked as an engineer all his life until he retired last April, everything had its place. Shelby knew he also enjoyed wood working, and seemed to have a tool for every kind of job.

Mr. T set up two sets of sawhorses, one for him and one for her. He also sorted through a bunch of his old tools and made her a complete set of her own. She was so excited she couldn't wait to get started.

"The first thing we need to do, Shelby, is figure out if we are going to paint or stain our project." Mr. T pondered the piles in front of him. "We bought some stain while we were at Baxter's Hardware Store but I also have a gallon of barn-red paint."

Shelby looked long and hard at the items they would be staining or painting. Try as she might, she couldn't guess what this surprise project might be. "Can we do half of them painted and half of them stained, Mr. T?" she asked.

"We sure can, Shelby," he patted her on the back and she knew she'd made a good choice. "Let's put six of the four-by-four oak posts on *my* sawhorses and six of the four-by-four oak posts on *your* sawhorses."

They picked up each post together, Shelby on one end and Mr. T on the other, until each set of sawhorses held six. They worked so well together Shelby didn't want the project to ever end.

"Since we got the oak posts exactly six feet tall and four-by-four around, we don't have to cut them down in size." Mr. T scratched his head. "But we do have to sand each one of them to make sure they are smooth and no one will get a splinter. Here's a sanding block for you and one for me. Hold it like this." He put it in her hand just so. "When we sand the posts we want to go with the grain of the wood, the long way down the post, and not side to side." He showed Shelby exactly what he meant. "Oh, and we have to wear safety glasses while we work. We don't want to get anything in our eyes."

Shelby watched, wide eyed, as Mr. T showed her how to sand the long posts. Then, she took her sanding block in hand, put a licorice rope in her teeth, and began on her posts. Slowly and industriously, she smoothed those posts down until there were no splinters to harm anyone. This made her smile, to think that her work could keep fingers safe. It made Mr. T smile, too. Before they knew it, after a few days, all those posts were smooth.

Chapter Eight

For the next couple of weeks, Shelby and Mr. T worked two hours every day in the garage on their project. After all, Shelby was a soon-to-be 5th grader who also wanted to have a little fun during her summer break in the water and in the sun. Mrs. and Mr. T also had errands to run during the week and usually took Shelby with them.

They shopped at the farmer's market, took trips to the post office, had doctor's appointments, and sometimes they even went on a surprise road trip to the next town to have lunch. Shelby thought some kids might have found this boring, but not her. This was normal and she loved it. She enjoyed going to town to visit the older people because they all knew her. Most of these people had watched her grow up over the years. She'd known them her entire life.

And each day, Shelby and Mr. T continued to work on their project.

"Now that we have all the sanding done on the main pieces, Shelby," said Mr. T, "we are going to make the bases. Let's put our ten two-by-four oak boards up on the sawhorses so that we can get some measurements before cutting them." Shelby helped Mr. T lift them up on the sawhorses. They were careful to place them flat next to each other.

"Shelby," he said, "I need help making sure my calculations are correct, so grab your note pad and pencil, please. Time to practice your engineering skills. We need four pieces of board for each of the twelve four-by-four oak posts we finished sanding. So tell me then, how many total pieces of board do we need?"

Shelby wrote down twelve for the posts they had, times four boards per post, and did a quick multiplication just like in school last year. "Forty-eight," she said, proud she'd done so well in math.

"That's right, Shelby," said Mr. T. "Let's do it again. If each board is ninety-six inches long right now, and we want to make each new board eighteen inches long, then how many boards will we get from each of these two-by-four oak boards?"

Again, Shelby wrote down ninety-six for the length of the boards, divided by eighteen for the inches each board would be. She did the calculation just like she would have in Mrs. Sappington's class. She was so excited when she was done she shouted out, "5.33 boards!"

"That's right Shelby. You are *so* smart." Mr. T gave her a big smile. Then he picked up a tape measure and pencil and showed Shelby how to measure the boards. He explained how to make them exactly eighteen inches long. Shelby took the tape measure and pencil and marked the remaining nine boards without any help at all. She even checked her boards against Mr. T's just to make sure her markings looked like his.

When she was all done with the little marks and felt she'd got them just right, she turned them into bigger lines so Mr. T could start cutting them.

"Shelby, can you hand me the square from the work bench, please?" asked Mr. T. "It's a triangle shaped piece of metal with a flat edge on it." Shelby looked around for a moment but couldn't find the triangle piece of metal. She lifted a bag of wooden knobs and there it was.

"Is this it, Mr. T?" asked Shelby.

"That's it," he said. Shelby watched closely as he marked stronger, thicker lines on the board to make it easier to cut to the correct lengths. Then he handed the triangle and marker to Shelby. Now it was her turn. Carefully, she made nice straight lines and then compared them to Mr. T's example. Before she knew it she was all done... and it was time for dinner.

Chapter Nine

Over the next several weeks, Shelby and Mr. T sanded all forty-eight of those boards to make sure they were smooth and splinter-free. Soon they would be ready to paint and stain.

Shelby listened to Mr. T tell her stories of when he was a kid, and made little projects with *his* grandpa. She learned that he really cherished those moments, and she understood now that Mr. T knew how his grandpa felt being able to teach someone so important to him. Memories are something you never forget, and she knew she would remember this time with Mr. T forever.

They spent hours in the garage talking about life, explaining or asking questions about the project they were making. Mrs. T always came to check on them or to tell them that lunch was ready, but she didn't want bother them too much, Instead, Mrs. T would often watch them from the screen

door, where she would chuckle quietly to herself. They painted and stained the boards according to their original plan until they were the perfect colors and shades, and they were like two best friends.

One day, Mr. T said, "Shelby, I think we are finally ready to start putting our little project together since we have all the hard work done."

Shelby was so excited as they gathered one four-by-four oak post, four two-by-four oak boards, screws, four decorative hangers, a drill, and some licorice and placed them on the workbench. Mr. T explained that they needed to make a base or "feet" for the four by four post to stand up straight and tall. She slipped on her safety glasses and helped hold the post in place while Mr. T pre-drilled the holes for each base. He handed Shelby the drill with a screwdriver bit and let her run the screws into the base to hold everything in place.

Shelby was so happy because after so many weeks of prepping, she would soon finally see the finished project. They got one wooden piece standing up straight on the ground and Shelby asked "What is it, Mr. T?"

Mr. T looked at her and shook his head. He said, "You'll have to wait and see, Shelby, but we can't move any further until the remaining pieces on the ground over there look like this. It's Friday, now, and you have the weekend to spend time with your parents. So, I'll see you next week when we get started again, alright, kiddo?"

Shelby was content with his answer, but tried with all her might to figure out what it was going to be. She wondered if maybe since they were making an even number of them, that maybe two of them would make a volleyball net or maybe a tetherball pole. "Guess I'll just have to wait and see," Shelby thought.

Chapter Ten

The next Monday morning, Shelby appeared at Mrs. and Mr. T's kitchen door bright and early. "Good morning Mr. and Mrs. T!" she said with a great big smile. "Mr. T and I have a busy week ahead of us putting our project together, and I can't wait to get started."

Shelby had been looking forward to Monday morning all weekend long. After working on this project two hours a day every single day for the past couple of months, she was finally going to understand what Mr. T had needed her help in making. A special thanks to Mrs. T for her yummy lunches and special afternoon home made snacks made each day.

"Well, come on Shelby, let's get our day started," said Mr. T, and just like that they were off to the garage. Over the next week they worked hard to pre-drill and put together the pieces of wood one by one.

By Friday afternoon Shelby still didn't have a clue as to what their project was. She looked at all twelve oak posts standing in the middle of the garage, each on their four feet, some painted a pretty barn red and some stained a beautiful medium oak. "Mr. T, I've thought about this all week and I still don't understand what these are supposed to be."

Mr. T smiled at her and shook his head. "Shelby, I still can't tell you — but! I promise you that by *next* week you'll understand, because we will have them completed and ready for delivery." Shelby nodded, but it still didn't keep her from wondering what these might be and where they were going to be delivered. She just couldn't figure it out.

Mrs. T popped into the garage. "Hey, you two - dinner's ready; and Shelby, your mom and dad will be here in ten minutes."

At dinner everyone laughed and talked, especially Shelby. She loved to tell stories and let her mom and dad know all about her day. Shelby had such positive people in her life, both family and friends. It was so wonderful that these friends included her in many of their daily activities of meal

planning, shopping, doctor's visits, and, most importantly, what coloring books Mr. and Mrs. T would color in. They were such good sports and played along when Shelby entertained them with her stories.

Shelby explained to her mom and dad that she and Mr. T were almost done with their project. "But you can't come into the garage and see it until they're completely done," she told her parents. "Oh," she frowned just a bit, "and I'm not quite sure what we're making but next week they should be done."

Mr. T smiled at Shelby's mom and dad. "Well, Shelby," said her mom, "I know most surprises are worth the wait, and so I know whatever you two are working on will be worth waiting for." She winked at Mr. T over Shelby's head.

As they headed out the door to go home, Shelby's dad asked Mr. T if he would see him next week at his doctor's appointment. "Yes doctor," said Mr. T with a grin, "at my regular check up. Good night."

Chapter Eleven

It was 7:00 AM on the dot.

"Well, look who's here bright and early. Good morning Shelby," said Mrs. T. Shelby had been too excited to wait any longer to go over to Mrs. and Mr. T's, because this was going to be a busy week. She would help Mr. T finish putting their project together, and he had a big doctor's appointment. "What would you like for breakfast?" asked Mrs. T.

Shelby thought for a moment. "Could I please have some cinnamon toast and a glass of chocolate milk? It's my favorite!" Mr. T came down the stairs and said, "I'll have exactly what Shelby is having, Mrs. T." He gave Shelby a big smile.

After breakfast they went into the garage to start working. "Alright Shelby," said Mr. T, "We need to put the finishing touches on our project. Let's get the decorative hooks and start placing them on each stand. We will need four hooks per hat rack." He glanced sideways at her to see if she was listening.

She was. "These are *hat racks*, Mr. T?!?" Shelby said with excitement.

So, finally, Mr. T explained to Shelby how after he was diagnosed with cancer he lost all his hair because of the treatments he was given. But no one had a hat he could borrow to cover his head to protect it from the sun. This made him think, and he decided that once he got well, he wanted to create hat racks full of hats to place in the hospital and cancer centers. Then, patients could borrow a hat to wear as they lost their hair, too.

"Now, I have two boxes full of hats I wore while I was going through treatment, and won't need them anymore - since my hair is growing back, I thought we could donate them by placing them on the hat racks."

Shelby was bowled over that Mr. T was not only taking time to do something so good for others, but that he in

her in his project. She listened while he explained his idea and what his plans were to deliver the hat racks full of hats.

"Next week, on August 20th," said Mr. T, "we will deliver the hats and hat racks to the hospitals. You and I will have a busy day, Shelby. Mrs. T will go with us since my doctor's appointment was changed to that day, early in the morning."

Shelby could hardly wait.

That evening at dinner, Shelby told her mom and dad their plans for next week. Shelby's mom and dad smiled at Mr. and Mrs. T as Shelby explained their upcoming day in detail.

Little did Shelby know that her mom and dad would have a part in presenting the hats and hat racks to the hospitals — something Shelby would soon find out and be so happy about. After all, it was almost time for school to start back up and Shelby would be sad not to be spending each day with Mr. and Mrs. T. But she would be happy to see her friends and teachers and tell them about her summer project.

Chapter Twelve

"Shelby, honey it's time to wake up," said her mom in a soft voice. "Today's an exciting day for you. You need to get going to Mr. and Mrs. T's house a little earlier so you can load everything up in his truck to deliver the hat racks, and so Mr. T can get to his doctor's appointment."

Shelby gave a big stretch and a yawn, then hopped out of bed and started getting ready. She picked out the prettiest little pink and green sundress to wear with cute matching sandals. Her mom combed her hair extra neat, and kissed both cheeks for "sparkle." Shelby giggled, then she gave her mom and dad a big hug and a kiss and headed to Mr. and Mrs. T's house.

Shelby's mom and dad stood on the front porch and watched their cheery, bubbly little girl make her way to

Mrs. and Mr. T's house. "We are so lucky to have a little girl like Shelby," said her dad. "She reminds me of you, so caring and compassionate towards others."

Her mom smiled and said, "If I may say so myself, she has great parents and wonderful people like Mr. and Mrs. T in her life. Guess we better get ready as we have a big day ahead of us too."

Shelby skipped up to Mrs. and Mr. T's house. "Good morning Mr. and Mrs. T! It's going to be a great day today… I just know it!" she said cheerfully.

Mr. T had already loaded up the hat racks in the back of the truck and secured them so they wouldn't fall out. Then all three of them climbed in the truck cab and headed to Mr. T's doctor's appointment.

Shelby pulled her favorite CD from her bag and placed it in the CD player. "Ok," she said, "everyone has to sing along…. 'I've got sunshine on a cloudy day. When it's cold outside I've got the month of May…' They sang and laughed the whole way to the doctor's office.

Inside the doctor's office, everyone welcomed Mr. and Mrs. T, but they especially welcomed Shelby. Since this was her dad's office they had watched her grow up over the years, but they had seen her a whole lot more during the last year because of all Mr. T's visits.

"Tom Tucker, are you ready?" asked Nurse Ashley, as she called Mr. T to go back to the examination room.

"Yes I am," said Mr. T, and he and Mrs. T and Shelby all walked back into the examination room and waited for Shelby's dad, Dr. John, to come in.

Knock knock!

"Good morning to my favorite people," said Dr. John as he came into the room. "I have some great news Tom…. your cancer is all gone." These were the words they were hoping for and so it truly was a great day. Shelby decided they needed a group hug and a high five to celebrate!

Chapter Thirteen

The time came to present the hat racks to the hospitals. As Mrs. and Mr. T and Shelby placed each hat rack inside the elevator to take up to the cancer floor, they saw Mr. Baxter from Baxter's Hardware. "Oh, we need to show him our project, Mr. T!" said Shelby.

"Maybe we'll see him in a few moments, Shelby," said Mr. T. "But for now we have to get all of these off the elevators so the visitors and patients can use them."

After they loaded the elevator they rode up several floors to the cancer level. The doors opened — and Shelby was so surprised to see hundreds of people waiting — for them! The room was so *full* of people: hospital staff, nurses and doctors, patients and their families, and several people wearing gold coats. There were even balloons and a big cake with punch, too.

Some of the staff helped them take the hat racks out of the elevator and move them to a designated location.

Shelby was so flabbergasted to see all of this. "Mr. T," she asked, "are they having a party for someone special?" Mr. T gave Shelby a big smile and said, "This is for the dedication of our project. And the party is for *you* too, Shelby." Shelby's mouth dropped open in a big "O."

Shelby's mom and dad came over from the crowd. "We can start whenever you are ready, Tom," said Shelby's dad. They all made their way over to a special podium. Over by the podium, Shelby recognized Dr. Davis, the CEO of Clarkson Cancer Hospital. He walked up and began to speak.

"Today is a very special day," said Dr. Davis. "Not only have we recently remodeled our cancer center, but we have a special dedication today to benefit our patients and our hospital. This-" he gestured to Mr. T "-is Tom Tucker. Tom has been an asset to our community and as a patient at our hospital, in ways we won't go into here, because it would take a bit too long!" There were chuckles in the audience. "Now, we would like to recognize his efforts in giving back. It is my understanding that he and a caring and compassionate little girl named Shelby Summers made something over the summer to benefit others while they receive medical treatment. Now, without further ado, I would like to introduce Dr. John Summers, to elaborate."

The crowd clapped and welcomed Shelby's dad to the podium. He cleared his throat and said "It is my honor and pleasure to be part of this special day. Not only has Tom been my patient, but he and his wife have been a huge piece of my family's life for many years. They have cared for our daughter, Shelby, since she was first born."

He smiled down at Shelby. "We have been honest and straightforward with Shelby about Tom's cancer prognosis and letting her know what to expect throughout this process. She has asked many questions and has been an instrumental piece in Tom's care and recovery. I would like to let Mr. Tom Tucker himself say a few words."

Shelby's dad stepped down from the podium and gave a big hug to both Mr. and Mrs. T. Then Mr. and Mrs. T took their turn at the podium.

Mr. T said, "I need Shelby to come up here with me, please." Shelby's heart pounded as she stepped up next to Mr. and Mrs. T and saw all those people in the crowd looking at her and smiling.

"This project couldn't have been done without Shelby's dedication and commitment to helping others," said Mr. T. "She has worked many hours helping me build these hat racks and she never complained one moment. She was a huge help to Mrs. T and I throughout my treatment, making a difficult time a little bit easier. I wanted to be able to give back to a community that gave so much to me and my wife. Your continued support, love, and offers of help made us realize why we love this community. Thank you for this day and thank you for taking such good care of me and my family over the last year. And, as of this morning, I learned that I am cancer free."

The crowd clapped and everyone smiled. Mr. T took Mrs. T and Shelby by the hand and began to walk off the stage. "Wait a moment, Tom," said Dr. Davis. "We have something special just for you."

Shelby noticed a rectangle shaped item covered with a while sheet. "Mr. Tucker and Shelby made twelve hat racks to donate to our cancer hospital. He *also* donated approximately forty hats for cancer patients to borrow as they go through their treatments. When they are done they simply return them for someone else to use. Because of this generous donation, the hospital will donate another forty hats to be used when this supply runs out."

Dr. Davis removed the white sheet and presented a shiny bronze plaque. "Mr. Tucker, on behalf of the Cancer Hospital we would like to present this plaque in your honor to be placed near the hat racks."

The crowd stood and clapped, giving Mr. T and Shelby their congratulations. Shelby saw the plaque was bronze with Mr. T's picture on it. Beneath his picture it said, "Tom T's Hat Rack," along with information about the hat racks.

The Chamber Ambassadors in their gold coats quickly gathered around the podium and stretched out a yellow ribbon to be cut for the dedication. Mr. T and Shelby were handed an enormous pair of scissors.

"We need your help," said one of the gold coated Ambassadors. "Can everyone help us say 'Tom T's Hat Rack?'" Everyone said it in unison. "Okay," the ambassador continued. "Smile…. Now cut!" and Mr. T and Shelby cut the ribbon.

The hospital's CEO, Dr. Davis, asked if Mr. T and Shelby would come back next week when the plaques were hung and the hat racks were placed to take a picture with them. Of course, it would have to be before Thursday, as that was the first day of school for Shelby.

On the way back home Shelby couldn't stop smiling or talking. She was so excited to be a part of this day and give back to her community.

"You know, Mr. T," she said, "it's sad that people have to go through bad things. But knowing there are great people who make it better for others makes me smile. You are one of those people, Mr. T. You went through a rough year and yet you always made time for our family. Then to do something great for others going through the same situation makes me so happy to have you and Mrs. T in my life!"

"Shelby," said Mr. T, "we are the lucky ones. You are a very special little girl that has always put others first. You have a beautiful smile that can light up a room. Do you remember when you went to my treatments with me, and by the time we left you could hear laughter coming from the other patients? That's something very special that not everyone else can do. You always look at things and think.... What can I do to help rather than asking what's in it for me? Thank you for caring so much, and I know you will do great things in life by starting so young."

Chapter Fourteen

"Good Monday morning to some of my favorite people!" said Shelby as she stood in the kitchen doorway of Mrs. and Mr. T's house. "You know, I've been thinking about last week."

"Oh?" said Mrs. T.

"I have been thinking about how great it was to make hat racks for the boys and men to wear, but what about the girls?" Shelby asked. "Most all of the hats are boy hats, and girls don't want to wear boy hats," she said with a funny face.

"That's a great point, Shelby," said Mrs. T. "Why don't you talk to Mr. T and see what you two can come up with?"

"That's a great idea, Mrs. T. Thank you." Shelby ran to the garage where Mr. T was. "What are you doing out here Mr. T?" she asked.

"I am cleaning up some of the leftover scraps of wood from our project," said Mr. T.

"Mr. T, I got to thinking about last week and the hat racks we made," she said. "I was thinking that it's a wonderful idea, but it's mainly for boys, not girls. Since girls go through cancer treatments too, they're going to go bald, but I don't think they want to wear boy hats."

Mr. T pulled up a chair to listen to Shelby. She continued, "I think we need to figure something out for the girls to choose from if they don't want to wear a hat. So I was thinking, what about a scarf rack?"

Mr. T smiled at her. "That's a great idea, Shelby. They would be easy to make, and I have enough material for six of them. It won't take long as they are simpler to make."

Over the next couple of days, Shelby and Mr. T worked hard to create six simple scarf racks to take to the hospital so that girls would have something to choose from if they didn't want to wear a hat. Again, Shelby and Mr. T laughed and talked while Mrs. T provided yummy lunches and snacks.

On Wednesday they loaded up the six scarf racks and headed to the cancer hospital. The hospital staff was

waiting for them, so when she and Mr. T arrived they had their picture taken next to one of "Tom T's Hat Racks" and got a special tour of where the other hat racks were located.

"Dr. Davis," Shelby said, "I have another surprise for you."

"Oh you do?" he asked. "Well, what is it Shelby?"

"I thought our idea of the hat racks was awesome," she said, "but those hats are kind of more for boys. What about the girls that are going through treatments? What if they don't want to wear boy hats? Well, Mr. T and I made scarf racks to donate to the hospital and place different colored scarves on for the girls to borrow."

"Shelby, you have to be the most thoughtful little girl I know," said Dr. Davis. "You are exactly right."

Mr. T and Shelby got the scarf racks from the truck and delivered them back up to Dr. Davis. Everyone at the hospital was surprised, because Shelby hadn't even told her mom or dad. At the end, Shelby handed Dr. Davis a Ziploc baggie holding $18.35. "This is my donation to get some scarves to put on the racks. I want to help get them started."

"Shelby," said Mr. T, "I'm so surprised you would consider using your allowance money to give to the hospital for scarves. How about we go to the store to see what scarves we can buy with that, and then let's see what we can find around the hospital."

"And Shelby," said Dr. Davis, "be sure and come back after school on Tuesday and see your scarf racks hung up."

"I sure will!" called Shelby.

As they were walking out to the truck, Mt. T said, "You always amaze me with your kindness, Shelby."

"Well," she said, "I learned from the best! When I get back to your house I need to borrow some notebook paper and a pencil. I need to write something for my teacher, ok, Mr. T?" He nodded and they drove home.

CHAPTER FIFTEEN

When Mr. T and Shelby got home, Shelby said, "Mrs. T, can I please borrow a notebook and a pencil?"

"Well sure you can, Shelby," said Mrs. T. "They are in the junk drawer in the desk. Help yourself."

Shelby found a brand new spiral notebook and a purple pencil with green smiley faces. She sat down at the kitchen table and began writing.

Later, Mrs. T asked, "Shelby you have been so focused on writing for the last half an hour. I haven't heard a peep out of you! What has you so focused?"

"I have a little bit of homework before school tomorrow and I almost forgot," said Shelby.

"Homework?" Mrs. T asked. "Shelby, school hasn't even started yet. How in the world can you have homework already?"

Shelby explained to Mrs. T how her 4th grade teacher, Mrs. Sappington, who was now going to be her 5th grade teacher *too*, had asked the students to write an essay on their summer break. The best story would be placed on the newly decorated bulletin board outside their classroom for a month.

Mrs. T smiled and went back to cooking dinner. Shelby had asked for roast beef and potatoes with gravy for dinner. Her favorite!

That night, after Shelby went to bed, her mom gathered Shelby's things together for her first day of school. In Shelby's papers she saw a story titled "A Summer I'll Never Forget," by Shelby Summers. Her mom couldn't help but read a few lines.

"This summer was so inspiring and creative, and I helped give back to a community I call home. A did a special project with a great person and it made a bad situation turn into a positive one that will benefit others. This summer has changed my life for the better."

Shelby's mom put the paper away and finished gathering Shelby's things. Her mom knew that Shelby would tell her all about whatever she was writing so there was no need to ask. Shelby would tell them about it when the time was right.

Chapter Sixteen

"Shelby, it's the first day of 5th grade," said her dad. "It's time to get up and get ready. You don't want to be late for school."

Shelby gave a yawn and a stretch and got up and started getting ready for school. She was excited because she would get to see her friends and hear all about their summer vacations. She loved all of her teachers and couldn't wait to see them too.

"See you tonight for dinner. Okay, Shelby?" said her mom.

Riiiiiiing went the school bell as Shelby skipped up the school's steps. She ran to her classroom.

"Good morning class," said Mrs. Sappington. "Welcome to your first day of 5th grade. I hope you all had a wonderful, relaxing, yet fun summer. Who took time to write an essay on your summer break?"

Several hands went in the air while other students rustled through their bags to find their essays.

"Please take a moment to pass them to the front of the classroom," said Mrs. Sappington. "I will grade them over the weekend. There will be three winning essays, and they will be placed on the bulletin board outside our classroom."

In between class and recess that day, Shelby went to see each of her previous teachers until she had seen them all. This was something she enjoyed doing every year. Next year she would be attending middle school and wouldn't be able to see them as often. So she was going to cherish this year.

On the bus ride home, she and the other girls talked and talked and talked until they got to Shelby's stop. "Bye everyone, see you tomorrow!" said Shelby.

Mr. and Mrs. T were waiting for Shelby when she got off the bus. "Hey Shelby," said Mr. T. "Dr. Davis called about an hour ago and asked us to swing by the hospital to see him when you got home from school."

"Okay, let's go," said Shelby, wondering what Dr. Davis had in mind. They all three jumped in the truck and headed to town. Shelby's mom and dad had to work late, so they decided they would have dinner in the hospital lounge with them.

When they arrived at the front desk it just so happened that Dr. Davis was walking by. "Well hello, Shelby," he said. "I'm so glad you got my message. I have something to show you. Come this way."

They walked down the hall and took the elevator to the cancer center. Across the hallway from the elevator door stood one of the hat racks with several great hats hanging from it. A big, shiny plaque was on the wall next to it with Mr. T's picture and a description of the "Tom T's Hat Rack."

"Well what do you think, Shelby?" said Dr. Davis. As Shelby got closer she saw her scarf rack next to the hat rack with a beautiful assortment of scarves hanging from it in all colors. Above the scarf rack it said 'Shelby's Scarves." Below this it said, 'Take One - Leave One.' Shelby was speechless. Her eyes lit up like it was Christmas, and she gave Dr. Davis a huge hug.

"It's perfect," she said. "Absolutely perfect, Dr. Davis." Shelby looked up at Mr. and Mrs. T to get their approval.

"We had a bunch of scarves from our little shop in the hospital that weren't being used," said Dr. Davis. "So we donated them on your behalf, Shelby. Your other five scarf racks are next to some of Tom T's Hat Racks. They belong together. Thank you so much for thinking of our patients that are going through treatment. This is something so beneficial, and now they don't have to worry about getting a scarf if they can't afford one."

Shelby had a permanent smile on her face the rest of the evening.

The next day at school Shelby was still beaming with joy. She saw Mrs. Gentry in the hallway. "Shelby," said Mrs. Gentry. "I can't tell you how much I have missed that beautiful grin all summer. Seeing it now reminds me how lucky we are to have you at our school. Did you have a good summer?"

"I had an amazing summer. Mr. T and I …." Riiiiiing went the school bell before Shelby could finish. "I've gotta go to

class Mrs. G. See you later." Shelby gave a big wave and ran to class.

Shelby didn't have time to visit all her past teachers as she had planned. Because she was in 5th grade now, they got started right away on their studies.

Riiiiiing went the last bell at the end of the school day.

"You boys and girls have a great weekend and I'll see you bright and early Monday morning," said Mrs. Sappington. Shelby quickly gathered her things, walked over to Mrs. Sappington, and gave her a hug. "You have a great weekend too, Mrs. Sappington!" She then caught up with her friends to head to the bus.

The girls talked non-stop on the bus home about their summer break while Shelby listened and giggled with them. She really enjoyed being around her friends again and loved hearing their stories. When the bus approached Shelby's stop she said " Bye girls… Have a great weekend and see you Monday!"

"Bye Shelby!" they all said in unison.

That same Friday afternoon, Mrs. Sappington called Shelby's mom. "Hi Karen, it's Mrs. Sappington, Shelby's 5th grade teacher," she said.

"Hi, Mrs. Sappington, what can I do for you?" Karen asked.

"I just wanted to tell you that it is such a pleasure to have Shelby in my class again this year. She truly is a sweet and kind little girl..." They talked for a little while longer and then hung up the phone.

Chapter Seventeen

Over the weekend, Shelby spent time with her family. One day they all went to the zoo along with Mrs. and Mr. T, Shelby had wanted to do this for a while, but it was tough to plan ahead with her mom and dad's schedule. It was a nice surprise for Shelby as she thought they had to work this weekend. She really enjoyed the time she got to spend with everyone together, and had so much fun watching the cheetahs, giraffes, and penguins.

Shelby got a chance to see the zoo's animal hospital and was really impressed. They had such great people helping the animals get better when they were sick and making sure the animals were current on their shots. The zoo staff had just brought in a baby panda to make sure it was healthy and to see how much it weighed. Shelby even got a chance to pet the baby panda, and it must have liked her, because it licked her cheek! It was so cute!

When they got back home they fixed dinner and listened to Shelby tell them all about the first couple of days of school. She told them about her friends' trips, her homework, and what things they would be doing this year in 5th grade.

"Shelby, time to wake up," said her dad early the next Monday morning. "It's a school day and you don't want to be late." Shelby rustled around and gave a yawn, then hopped out of bed and started getting ready for school. Shelby's mom had a quick breakfast waiting for her.

"How did you know cinnamon toast was my favorite, mom?" Shelby asked. Her mom just smiled.

"Hope you have a great day at school Shelby. I love you," said her mom as Shelby headed out the door.

Shelby and her dad visited for a bit in the yard, and then Shelby headed to Mr. and Mrs. T's house to say good morning. "Bye, dad, love ya!" she yelled while skipping down the driveway.

"Bye, Shelby, love you too," whispered her dad.

"Good morning Mr. and Mrs. T," said Shelby in the kitchen doorway. Then they all went to the bus stop. As it pulled up she waved to them and said, "I'll see you both tonight."

Shelby and her friends picked right back up on their conversation from after school on Friday. They got to school and headed to the gym for their "Monday Morning Message."

"Good morning students," said Mrs. Gentry. "I hope you are all ready for your first full week of school, as we are excited to get this school year started. This morning, we have something special to tell you about one of our students."

Mrs. Sappington came up onto the stage as the 301 students sat quietly. "Good morning, students," she said.

"Good morning, Mrs. Sappington," said all the students together.

"At the end of last year I knew I was going to be teaching 5th grade to my then-4th graders," she said. "I asked them to write an essay about something they did over the summer that impacted them in a positive way. I received twenty essays out of twenty-four students. I had the pleasure, along with Mrs. Gentry, to read and choose the top three essays. We had one of them that really stood out and we want to share it all with you."

Mrs. Sappington read from a piece of paper:

"This summer was inspiring and creative, and I helped give back to a community I call home. A special project with a wonderful person made a bad situation turn into a positive one that will benefit others greatly. This summer has changed my life for the better."

"I feel my job is to help others in a way that is uplifting, caring, and comes 100% from the heart. Cancer is a word that we don't often talk about, yet it effects each one of us somehow. Someone very special to me was affected by this disease, and I pledged to help him fight it and show him he was not alone in this battle.

"I got to help with a project called 'Tom T's Hat Rack' and constructed and donated twelve hat racks along with forty hats to the cancer hospital. This will allow other people going through treatment and losing their hair to benefit from some really cool Mr. T inspired hats. Because these hats are not offered at the hospital, it was a way we could make a positive difference in the lives of others who are going through a tough time. It will give them hope that they will be able to donate the hat back when they are done with it.

"I helped with this project because I wanted to give back to a great community. What's in it for me? The satisfaction that I helped construct and donate these hat racks and to know that others greatly appreciate them. In life we must not hold our hand out and ask, "What's in it for me?" but rather ask, "What can I do for others?"

Mrs. Sappington looked at Shelby and motioned her to come stand next to her. Everyone started clapping as Shelby walked up onto the stage.

"This young lady here is the author of this story," said Mrs. Sappington. "It is because of her dedication, compassion, and big heart that she is standing up here on this stage." Shelby was beaming with joy — and then she couldn't believe her eyes! Mom, Dad, and Mrs. and Mr. T were all standing in the gym watching, too!

"I want you all to ask yourself this question every single day," Mrs. Sappington said. "What can you do for someone else today that will impact them in a positive way?"

Everyone started clapping again, and Mrs. Gentry said, "Shelby, thank you. Your story will not be placed near your classroom but rather on the big board outside our main office for *everyone* to see."

Shelby was so happy. She quickly ran down to give her parents a big hug. She also gave a big hug to Mrs. and Mr. T and just couldn't believe they were here!

Shelby had learned from great people how to have a positive outlook in life. Often, people that have bad things happen to them choose to focus on the negative things like, "Why me?" or "What did I do to deserve this?"

For Shelby, that wasn't an option. She took the bad and focused on the good. "What can I do to help?" she thought. She didn't do things for recognition, she did them because they came from her heart. She had always been told to treat others as you want them to treat you and always give respect.

Shelby was very proud of the things she had done, but the thing she was most proud of was her family. With her family's support there wasn't anything she couldn't do.

Pay it Forward

What can you do to help others in your community?

List some ways you can help - big or small - it doesn't really matter as long as you are doing something positive to help others.

1.

2.

3.

4.

5.

ABOUT THE AUTHOR

My good friend, Tom Trabue, was diagnosed with Hodgkin's Lymphoma earlier this year. To watch Tom go through chemotherapy and radiation, yet always remaining so positive, was such an inspiration. A long time ago, I decided to live my life by paying it forward to others as often as I could and try to encourage others to do simple acts of kindness for random strangers — it truly makes my heart happy.

I began writing this book in my head with those two inspirations. I have always wanted to write and publish a book, this year I felt compelled to do so and turned my dream into a reality. While on vacation in Montrose, Colorado, I had to get this book out of my head and onto paper!

One of the ways I've chosen to pay it forward is to become a Partner in Education with Midway Heights Elementary School in Columbia, MO, back in 2008. As a Partner in Education, I wanted to reach out to the students at our partner school and encourage *them* to do something good for someone else and pay it forward - hence, this book. Little did I know "Pay It Forward" is the overall school theme for the Columbia Public Schools for the 2012-2013 year!

Coincidence? I'm not so sure! And now I look forward to hearing all your stories of how this book inspired you to pay it forward, as well.

About the Illustrator

A native of Kansas City, Peggy A. Guest majored in Fine Art at Christian College, University of Missouri-Columbia, Kansas City Art Institute and Park University. She graduated in 1976, and began working , as an illustrator, for the Department of Defense, (Air Force Communications Command) at Richards-Gebaur Air Force Base in Kansas City. She transferred to the Department of the Army, and worked for several years at Ft. Leavenworth, Kansas in the Media Support Center. She was promoted to Writer/Editor for the Army Recruiting Command in Kansas City, until transferring to USDA's Crop Insurance Program in 1983, as a graphics/printing supervisor. Moving to Mid-Missouri in 1989, Guest and her husband started Guest Design Studio, in 1992. The studio provides clients with design, murals, fine art painting, sculpture, exhibits and displays and special projects. Guest is currently painting murals in Fayette, Missouri to promote the town's businesses. She was listed in Who's Who in American Women Artists in 2000. She and her husband, Joe, live and work in their studio outside Fayette, Missouri.

Visit her at www.PeggyGuest.com

Please Join Us!

We want to inspire others around the world to "Pay It Forward" and it starts with you!

On the following pages, we have provided the plans and directions on how to make your own hat rack!

We'd love to hear from you if this story has inspired you to make a hat rack and donate it to a cancer center in your community, or anything else that this book as inspired you to do, to give back to your community in a positive way.

You can have your mom, dad, grandparent, aunt or uncle e-mail a picture and story of you with something you made or something you did to benefit others, including what inspired you and where it will go (cancer center, local hospital, etc.), to:

info@michelespry.com

or have them post this information on our Facebook page at:

www.facebook.com/SPRYPublishing

Thank you for reading this story!

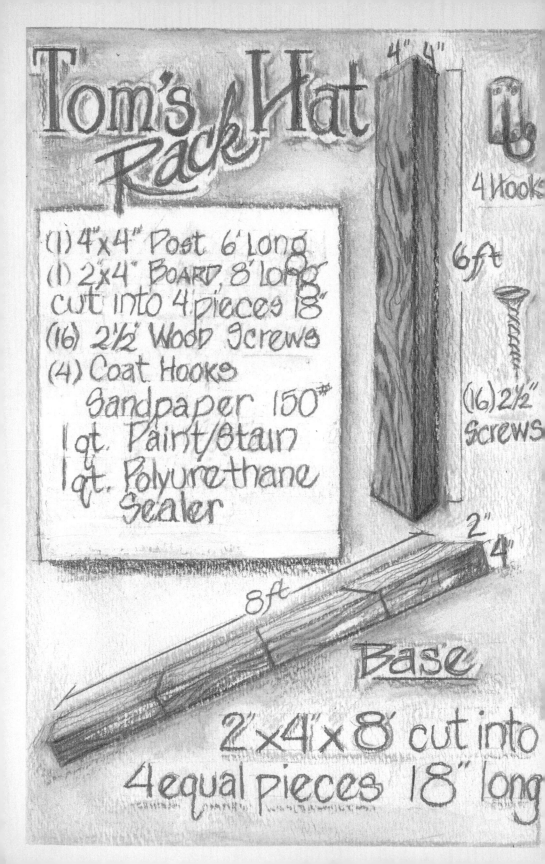

Tom's Hat Rack

(1) 4"x4" Post 6' Long
(1) 2"x4" Board, 8' Long
cut into 4 pieces 18"
(16) 2½" Wood Screws
(4) Coat Hooks
     Sandpaper 150#
1 qt. Paint/Stain
1 qt. Polyurethane
     Sealer

4" 4"

4 Hooks

6ft

(16) 2½" Screws

2"

4"

8ft

Base

2"x4"x8' cut into
4 equal pieces 18" long

DIRECTIONS

Sand Post smooth)
Cut (4) feet, 18" long, from
2x4'. Round over one
Corner of each Board
Sand Feet Smooth.
Screw Feet to Base of
Post, Rounded corners
Up.

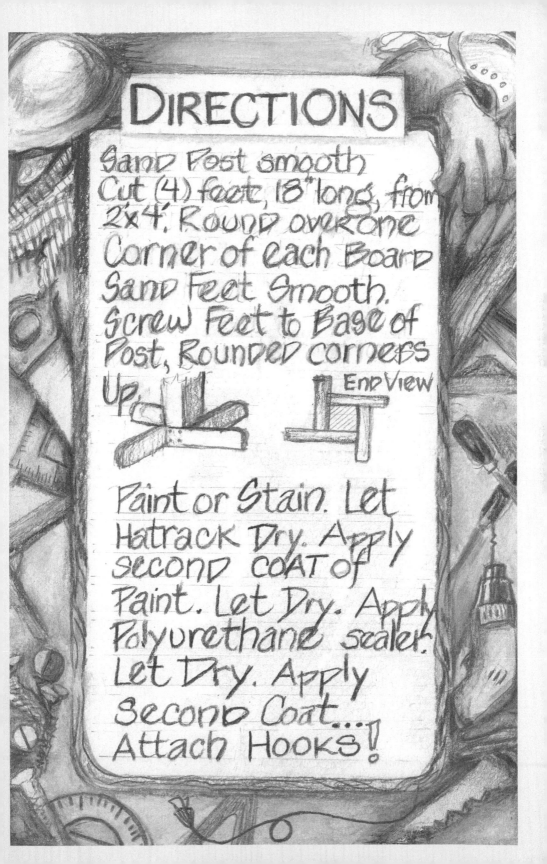

End View

Paint or Stain. Let
Hatrack Dry. Apply
second COAT of
Paint. Let Dry. Apply
Polyurethane sealer.
Let Dry. Apply
second Coat...
Attach Hooks!

CPSIA information can be obtained at www.ICGtesting.com
Printed in the USA
LVOW010527110113

315331LV00003B/7/P

9 780988 778238